Welcome to Miffy's World!

Based on the work of **Dick Bruna**
Story written by **R. J. Cregg**

SIMON SPOTLIGHT

New York   London   Toronto   Sydney   New Delhi

SIMON SPOTLIGHT
An imprint of Simon & Schuster Children's Publishing Division
1230 Avenue of the Americas, New York, New York 10020
This Simon Spotlight paperback edition January 2017
Published in 2017 by Simon & Schuster, Inc. Publication licensed by Mercis Publishing bv, Amsterdam.
Stories and images are based on the work of Dick Bruna.
'Miffy and Friends' © copyright Mercis Media bv, all rights reserved.
All rights reserved, including the right of reproduction in whole or in part in any form.
SIMON SPOTLIGHT and colophon are registered trademarks of Simon & Schuster, Inc.
For information about special discounts for bulk purchases, please contact Simon & Schuster Special Sales
at 1-866-506-1949 or business@simonandschuster.com.
Manufactured in the United States of America 1216 LAK
10 9 8 7 6 5 4 3 2 1
ISBN 978-1-4814-6773-5 (pbk)
ISBN 978-1-4814-6774-2 (eBook)

Miffy is a sweet little bunny. She lives in a small white house in a big bright world. Welcome to Miffy's world!

Miffy lives with Mummy and Daddy.
They eat breakfast together so Miffy
will be ready for all her adventures,
both big and small.

Miffy loves to play outside with her friends. She rides her bike with Melanie and Grunty. Even Snuffy the dog comes along! "Woof, woof!" Snuffy barks.

Melanie is Miffy's best friend. They play games together, like tennis. "Keep hitting it high, Melanie!" calls Miffy as they play.

"Okay!" says Melanie.

Grunty is Miffy's youngest friend. Sometimes Grunty needs a little extra help, but she can always play too! "I can do it!" says Grunty as she bowls with Melanie and Miffy.

Miffy goes to school with her friends. From math to reading, they learn something new each day. Some days they even play music for their teacher!

Miffy's class goes on field trips.
  "Cheep, cheep!" say the chicks when Miffy's class
visits the farm. The chicks are so cute and little!

Miffy likes to explore the library. There is so much to discover in every book. Sometimes Aunt Alice works as the librarian. Miffy wants to put books on the shelves. "Always happy to have some help!" says Aunt Alice.

On very special days Uncle Pilot visits Miffy at her house.
"Hello, Uncle Pilot!" Miffy calls.
"Hello Miffy!" he says from his airplane.

**Uncle Pilot takes Miffy on plane rides up in the sky.
Everything looks so small from above!**

Uncle Pilot brings Miffy gifts from faraway places.
"What is my surprise, Uncle Pilot?" asks Miffy.
"It's inside this box," says Uncle Pilot.
"Oh, I love surprises!" says Miffy.
Uncle Pilot has brought Miffy a dragon fruit. It tastes delicious!

Sometimes Miffy gets to go on visits. She loves going to Grandma and Grandpa's house. They are Daddy's mother and father.

Grandma shows Miffy how to find shapes in the clouds. "What does that one look like?" asks Grandma. "A sheep!" says Miffy.

Grandpa takes Miffy sailing in his boat. Daddy and Grandma come along! *"Sail, sail, sail, I'm sailing on the sea,"* they all sing. *"Sail, sail, sail, will you come and sail with me?"*

Boris and Barbara are also Miffy's friends. Boris gives Barbara beautiful flowers to show that he cares. Boris and Barbara love each other very much.

Boris works in a workshop with wood and tools. "What would you like to build, Miffy?" Boris asks. He helps Miffy make fun new things.

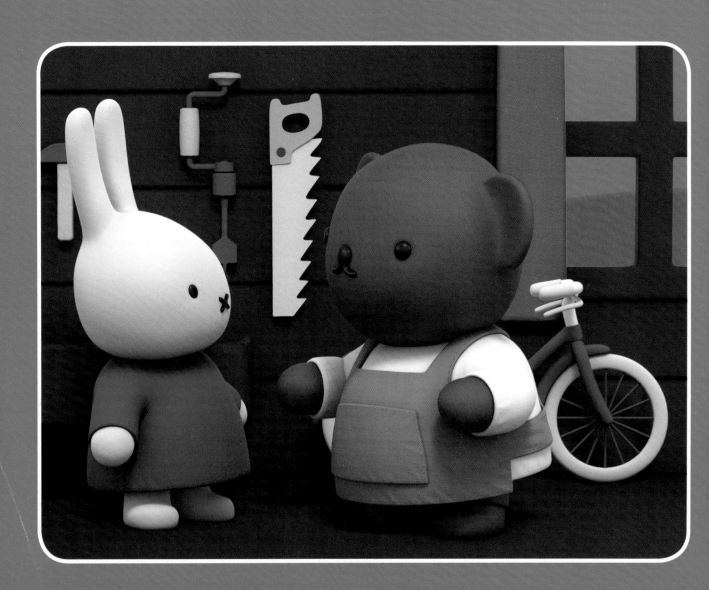

Barbara works in a shop where she sells fruits and vegetables. "What would you like to buy, Miffy?" asks Barbara. Everything looks so yummy!

In Miffy's world everyone works together to make each day an adventure!